TO NORTH POLE

BIG STONES AND ROX

BEE TREE

RABBITS FrENDS AND RALEtIONS

MY HOUSE

OWLS HOUSE

100 AKER WOOD

EEYORES GLOOMY PLACE

RATHER BOGGY AND SAD

IN 100 AKER WOOD

First published in Great Britain 2003
By Egmont Books Limited
239 Kensington High Street, London W8 6SA
Illustrated by Andrew Grey
Based on the 'Winnie-the-Pooh' works
By A.A. Milne and E.H. Shepard
© 2003 Disney Enterprises, Inc.
Designed by Clare Doughty
Edited by Catherine Shoolbred
Design © 2003 Egmont Books Limited
All Rights Reserved.

1 3 5 7 9 10 8 6 4 2

ISBN 1 4052 0526 1

Printed in Singapore.

Tigger Is Unbounced

One hot summer's day, Rabbit was talking to Pooh and Piglet. Pooh wasn't really listening. From time to time, he opened his eyes to say "Ah!"

Rabbit said, "You see what I mean, Piglet," and Piglet nodded to show that he did.

"In fact," said Rabbit, "Tigger's getting so Bouncy nowadays that it's time we taught him a lesson. Don't you think so, Piglet?"

Piglet agreed Tigger was very Bouncy and if they
could think of a way of unbouncing him, it would be
a Very Good Idea.

"What do *you* say, Pooh?" asked Rabbit.

Pooh opened his eyes and said, "Extremely."

"Extremely what?" asked Rabbit.

"What you were saying," said Pooh. "Undoubtably."

"But how shall we do it?" asked Piglet. "What sort of a lesson?"

"That's the point," said Rabbit.

"What were we talking about?" asked Pooh.

Piglet explained they were trying to think of a way to get the bounces out of Tigger, because however much you liked him, you couldn't deny it, he did bounce.

"Oh, I see," said Pooh. He tried to think, but he could only think of something which didn't help at all.

So he hummed it very quietly to himself.

If Rabbit
  Was bigger
And fatter
  And stronger,

or bigger
Than Tigger,

If Tigger was smaller,

Then Tigger's bad habit
Of bouncing at Rabbit

Would matter
No longer,

If Rabbit
  Was taller.

"I've an idea!" said Rabbit. "We take Tigger for a long explore and we lose him. The next morning we find him again and he'll be a **different Tigger** altogether. He'll be a Humble Tigger,
a Sad Tigger,
a Melancholy Tigger,
a Small and Sorry Tigger,
an *Oh-Rabbit-I-am-glad-to-see-you* Tigger.
That's why."

"I should hate him to go on being Sad," said Piglet.
"Tiggers never go on being Sad," explained Rabbit.
"But if we can make Tigger feel Small and Sad just for **five minutes**, we shall have done a **good deed.**"
So the only question was, where should they **lose** Tigger?

"We'll take him to the **North Pole**," said Rabbit.
"It was a **long explore** finding it, so it will be a
very long explore for Tigger **un**-finding it again."
Pooh felt glad. It was he who had first found the
North Pole so when they got there, Tigger would see
a notice saying,

and Tigger would then know what sort of bear he
was. **That** sort of bear. So it was arranged that they
would start the next morning and Rabbit would go
and ask Tigger to come.

The next day was quite a different day. Instead of being sunny, it was **cold and misty**. Pooh felt sorry for the bees who wouldn't be making honey on such a day. Piglet wasn't thinking of that, but of how **cold and miserable** it would be being lost **all day and night** on top of the Forest on such a day.

Rabbit said it was just the day for them. As soon as Tigger bounced out of sight, they would hurry in the other direction, and he would never see them again.

"Not never?" said Piglet, worriedly.

"Well, not until we find him again," said Rabbit. "Come on. He's waiting for us."

At Kanga's house, they found Roo waiting for them too. This made things Very Awkward.

Rabbit whispered behind his paw to Pooh, "Leave this to me!"

"Roo had better not come today," he said to Kanga. "He was coughing earlier."

"Oh Roo, you never told me," said Kanga, reproachfully.

"It was a biscuit cough," said Roo, "Not one you tell about."

"I think not today, dear. Another day," Kanga said.

"Ah, Tigger! There you are!" said Rabbit, happily. "All ready? Come on."

So they went.

At first Pooh and Rabbit and
Piglet walked together, and
Tigger ran round them
in circles. Then, when the
path got narrower, Rabbit,
Piglet and Pooh walked one

after another, and Tigger ran round them in oblongs.

When the gorse got very
prickly, Tigger ran up
and down in front of
them, and sometimes
bounced into Rabbit.
As they got higher, the

mist got thicker, so Tigger kept disappearing, and then
bouncing back again.
Rabbit nudged Piglet.
"The next time," he said.
"Tell Pooh."
"The next what?" said Pooh.
Tigger appeared,
bounced into Rabbit
and disappeared again.

"Now!" said Rabbit.
He jumped into a hollow
and Pooh and Piglet
jumped in after him.

The Forest was silent.
They could see nothing
and hear nothing.

Then they heard
Tigger pattering
about.

"Hallo?"
he said.

Then they
heard him
pattering
off again.

They waited a little longer and then Rabbit got up. "Well!"
he said proudly. "Just as I said! Come on, let's go!"
They all hurried off, with Rabbit leading the way.
"Why are we going along here?" said Pooh.
"Because it's the way home!" said Rabbit.
"I *think* it's more to the right," said Piglet, nervously.
They went on. "Here we are," said Rabbit, ten
minutes later. "No, we're not . . ."

"It's a funny thing," said Rabbit, another ten minutes later, "how everything looks the same in a mist. Lucky we know the Forest so well, or we might get lost."

Piglet sidled up to Pooh from behind.

"Pooh!" he whispered.

"Yes, Piglet?"

"Nothing," said Piglet, taking Pooh's paw. "I just wanted to be sure of you."

When Tigger had finished waiting for the others to catch him up, and they hadn't, he decided he would go home. Kanga gave him a basket and sent him off with Roo to collect fir-cones.

Tigger and Roo threw pine cones at each other until they had quite forgotten what they came for. They left the basket under the trees and went back for dinner.

Just as they were finishing dinner, Christopher Robin put his head around the door and asked,

"Where's Pooh?"

Tigger explained what had happened and Christopher Robin realised Pooh, Piglet and Rabbit were **lost in the mist** on the top of the Forest.

"It's a funny thing about Tiggers," Tigger whispered to Roo, "they **never** get lost."

"Well," said Christopher Robin to Tigger, "we shall have to go back and find them."

Rabbit, Pooh and Piglet were having a rest in a
sand-pit. Pooh was **rather tired** of the sand-pit,
because whichever direction they started in, they
always ended up at it again.

"Well," said Rabbit after a while. "We'd better get on.
Which way shall we try?"

"How about we leave," said Pooh, "and as soon as we're
out of sight of the sand-pit, we try to find it again?"

"What's the good of that?" asked Rabbit.

"Well," said Pooh, "we keep looking for Home and
not finding it, so if we looked for this pit, we'd be
sure not to find it, and we might find something
we *weren't* looking for, which might be just what
we were looking for really."

"Try," said Piglet to Rabbit, suddenly. "We'll wait
here for you."

Rabbit walked into the mist.

After Pooh and Piglet had waited twenty minutes for him, Pooh got up.

"Let's go home, Piglet," he said. "There are twelve pots of honey in my cupboard, and they've been calling to me for hours. I couldn't hear them because Rabbit would talk, but if nobody is saying anything then I shall know where they are. Come on."

They walked off together. For a long time Piglet said nothing, then suddenly he made a squeaky noise because now he began to know where he was. Just when he was getting sure, there was a shout and out of the mist came Christopher Robin.

"Oh! There you are," said Christopher Robin
carelessly, trying to pretend he hadn't been anxious.
"Here we are," said Pooh.
"Where's Rabbit?" asked Christopher Robin.
"I don't know," said Pooh.
"Oh – well, I expect Tigger will find him. He's sort of
looking for you all," said Christopher Robin.
"Well," said Pooh, "I've got to go home for *something* and
so has Piglet, because we haven't had it yet, and –"
"I'll come and watch you," said Christopher Robin.

So he went home with Pooh and watched him for some time.

All the time Christopher Robin was watching Pooh, Tigger was tearing around the Forest making loud yapping noises for Rabbit. And at last, a very Small and Sorry Rabbit heard him. And the Small and Sorry Rabbit rushed through the mist at the noise, and it suddenly turned into Tigger:

a Friendly Tigger,

a Grand Tigger,

a Large and Helpful Tigger,

a Tigger who bounced, if he bounced at all, in just the beautiful way a Tigger ought to bounce.

"Oh Tigger, I am glad to see you," cried Rabbit.

THIS STORY TOOK PLACE